Santa's Disastrous Delivery!

By
Glyn Davies

Copyright © 2023 by Glyn Davies

All rights reserved, no part of this book may be used or reproduced in any form whatsoever without written permission except in the case of brief quotations in critical articles or reviews

This book is a work of fiction. No names characters, businesses, organisations, places, events, and incidents either are the product of the authors imagination or are used fictitiously. any resemblance to actual persons, living or dead, events, or locales is entirely coincidental

Printed in the UK

For more information, contact:

glyngregdavies@gmail.com

www.glyndaviesbooks.com

Book design by Glyn Davies

Cover design by Robin Davies

ISBN- paperback **979-8370974069**

ISBN- Kindle B0BR8GJNV2

ISBN- Audible A2VBFZRDTYBLVD

First edition 2023

It was a lovely clear night with a fresh covering of new snow on the ground and all around, there was an air of freshness and excitement.

For it was Christmas Eve and Santa was on his way.

The Robinsons were all tucked up in bed and Kevin and Katie had hung up their stockings, and Mum and Dad had put everything ready for Santa's coming and were now all fast asleep.

They lived in a cottage on a hill overlooking a small village whose lights could be seen twinkling in the distance.

The Taylors, who lived next door were away, so they were looking forward to a quiet Christmas.

The night air was crisp and all around the stars were sparkling, when early in the morning a shooting star shot through the sky over the valley leaving a trail of stardust which fell over the houses.

This was no ordinary star, it was Santa's star, which meant that everybody would be fast asleep when he arrived.
Well nearly everybody.

Two policemen, Ken and Bill who were out on patrol in their police car, had been on the other side of the valley checking empty houses when Santa's star came over and they had missed the stardust.
This was going to be a night to remember
for a long time to come.

The Robinsons garden was well lit by the light of the moon
A snowman Kevin and Katie had made, stood on guard in the middle of the lawn.
Katie had put a pair of Dads old sunglasses on him,
so he looked a cool dude.

Over by the fishpond, Norman the concrete gnome sat fishing while Nobby the gnome stood with his hands on his hips, laughing the way he had done for the past four years when Katie had bought him home from the garden center.

A young rabbit came hopping into the lane looking for food and someone to play with when he suddenly stopped.

He pricked his ears up and sniffed the air twitching his nose, then he suddenly ran off towards his burrow and safety.

For in the distance a far-off strange sound could be heard coming from the valley.

A faint jingle of bells and the sound of chattering voices was slowly growing louder.

Then suddenly there was a SWHOOSH and Santa's sleigh came hurtling towards the Robinsons house.

It shot past, did a sharp turn round and came skidding onto

the roof with Santa pulling wildly on the reigns and all the reindeer digging their hooves in trying to stop.

As they did, they slid along the roof and finally stopped. Rudolph's nose hit the chimney and all the other reindeer skidded and crashed into the back of him.

The reindeer all shouted as heads and feet and antlers stuck into each other's bottoms.

"Oooh ugh aargh! Watch where you're sticking your antlers."

Rudolph at the front could be heard shouting,

 "oooh my poor doze, not again!"

No wonder it was always red.

While all this was going on, Santa at the back was thrown out of his sleigh.

He fell onto the roof which he rolled down and fell off

into a large snow drift, with a dull pluff.

He got up and brushed off the snow and pulled his tunic straight.

Santa looked up at the roof.

"Well done lads, that was quite a good landing that time."

Rudolph was rubbing his sore nose and Blitzson was still protesting that Comet had jabbed him in the bum on purpose.

"Hey, chill out man it's cool," said Comet.

"No, it's not" said Blitzson, "It's painful."

"I told you the old fool had drunk too many of those sherries people leave for him," said Cupid.

"Well, he can't leave them or the mince pies, people would be upset," said Donner.

"It's me that should be upset, I have to go behind Donner every year!" said Blitzson.

"I can't help it, it's all those mince pies he keeps giving us."

Brump, "Pardon me!" said Donner.

"That's what I mean" said Blitzson.

"Hey chill out man," said Comet.

"OH, shut up the lot of you" said Cupid,

"It's bad enough keeping that old fool out of trouble,

without looking after you lot!"

Brump, "I can't help it," said Donner.

By this time, Santa had looked round and decided

the best way in, as it was too dangerous down the chimney,

and in any case, most houses didn't have a chimney now,

it was all central heating.

He shouted up to Eric, his little elf who helped

with the parcels.

Eric took all the gifts and put them into the sack and threw

them down to Santa.

Which hit him on the head and knocked him over.

"Good shot," said Prancer.

"Right on target" said Dancer, then they both laughed.

"Sorry" said Eric, "You alright?"

"Yes, yes" said Santa, "I'm getting used to it now!"

Santa picked up the sack and looked up again.

"Eric, what's the magic word to get inside?"

"Holly Oaks," said Eric

Then went back to sorting out the back of the sleigh.

Santa stood back and closed his eyes and said the magic word, with a little plop he disappeared.

Immediately there was a terrible crash, bang, clang, clatter, bang, thump. "Oh aargh", clatter, tinkle, "Ooh ouch".

Then silence, before a muffled "Let me out!"

Cupid looked down.

"Where are you?" said Cupid.

"I'm in the tool shed" came the reply.

"Good grief," said Cupid.

He nodded his antlers and Santa came back with a plop.

"What was that word again?" "Holly oaks," said Eric.

"Oh, ha, I thought you said holey socks!"

"Hey man, that's cool, holey socks, I can dig that!"

"Shut up you idiot" said Blitzson.

"That's it, you tell him", said Prancer.

Brump went Donner!

"Oh, my poor doze," said Rudolph.

Brump went Donner!

"Cor, leave it out, will you?" said Blitzson.

Brump, "Sorry I can't help it," said Donner.

"Has anybody got an aspirin,

I'm getting one of my headaches?" said Cupid.

"Has anybody got a peg for my nose?" said Blitzson.

While this was going on, Santa was busily trying to get inside again.

He shut his eyes and thought hard, then with a "puff" he'd gone.

Santa found himself in a small room.

"This is a funny room" he thought,

"Not enough room for a bed."

He went to move and then realised

that he was in the bathroom.

With one foot down the toilet, he looked down.

"Silly me" he thought and pulled his foot out with a squelch,

immediately lost balance and fell forward into the bath.

Grabbing hold of the shower curtain on the way and pulling it on top of him with a crash, as the soap, bubble bath, shampoo and a yellow plastic duck scattered out on the floor.
He pulled himself out and found his way out & onto the landing. Looking into their rooms,
 Kevin and Katie were fast asleep.
Santa smiled and made his way downstairs to the lounge where the Christmas tree was.
By the open fire, on a table was a small plate with a mince pie and a small glass of sherry.
 He picked up the mince pie and put it into his pocket, "Donner will like that," he thought.
He drank the sherry and put the glass back on the table. Then knocked the table over with his sack as he turned around to go over to the tree.

"Oops clumsy me" said Santa, he dropped his sack onto the floor to pick up the table.

Unfortunately, Tibbs the cat was asleep in the same spot "Meeoooow" went Tibbs and shot out from under his sack, took one look at this funny man in a red suit and white beard in the house at 5 o'clock in the morning and went wild.

Tibbs ran up the curtains, jumped off onto the bookshelf bringing down lots of decorations and shot out the room and out through the cat flap.

Comet watched Tibbs scoot off up the lane
at warp factor three, he just said, "Far out man!"
Dancer and Prancer looked at each other and giggled.
"Things are going well by the look of it!" said Dancer.

Back in the lounge Santa took out all the presents and placed them under the tree, then picked up the empty sack.

"Right, how do I get out?" he thought.

He closed his eyes and thought the magic word, he opened his eyes, and he was still in the room.

The only trouble was a large fluffy pink elephant was in the room with him.

"Not the right word" he said to himself "But I'm sure they will like it."

He closed his eyes and thought again. He opened his eyes, the pink elephant was now sitting in an armchair and there was a wishing well in the middle of the lounge floor.

"Perhaps they could make a feature of it," he thought

"Right this time," he opened his eyes, there was now an eight foot stuffed bear standing in the corner,

wearing a lamp shade.

The elephant had been joined by a sea lion,

and Mrs. Robinsons expensive Chinese rug

was now a flower bed!

Santa thought he had better leave by the front door and let

Cupid sort it all out.

But unfortunately, the door from the lounge was blocked by a

huge Christmas pudding!

He looked round the room and decided that the window was

his only escape!

****

On the other side of the valley, two policemen. Ken and Bill

were patrolling their patch.

It had been a quiet night and they were looking forward to

going home for Christmas with the family.

"We had better check on Mr. and Mrs. Taylors place up at Sandy Lane

Their burglar alarms been going off lately for no reason."

"Righto" said Bill, "Then back to the station for a cup of tea"

Ken turned into Sandy Lane and drove slowly down towards Rose cottages.

"Stop the car!" shouted Bill.

"What's the matter?" said Ken.

"There look, coming out the Taylors window the crafty devil!"

"I still don't know what you mean," said Ken.

"That burglar dressed as Santa Claus! Right, you park the car, I'll go and arrest him."

Bill jumped out the car and carefully made his way over to the window so he didn't scare him off.

Santa was nearly out of the window

when a voice behind him said

"Here let me help you!"

"O thank you young man, that's very kind."

Santa looked round and saw a policeman.

"Caught in the act," said Bill.

"Ah well I suppose I have," laughed Santa.

"You're not supposed to see me you know!"

"Yes, I know that it's unfortunate for you we came along!" said Bill.

"Oh, I don't know, you could probably help me get some of the things out of the lounge!" said Santa,

"I've just got to call Eric on the roof."

"Well, I admire your cheek," said Bill.

Just then Ken came over. "Got him then?" said Ken.

"Yes, and his mate Eric is up on the roof,

stealing the TV aerial, I suppose!"

Santa suddenly realised that they thought he was a burglar.

"No, no you don't understand, I'm Santa Claus

Eric is my little elf helper."

"Yes of course you are, I'm Snow White and this is one of

my seven dwarfs!" said Bill pointing to Ken.

"You're nicked!" said Ken.

"What, no I'm not Nick, I just told you I'm Santa Claus."

"Right, I've got Santa you go and get Eric"

said Ken laughing.
Bill looked up at the roof and shouted

"Ok Eric we've got your mate, so come down quietly."

Brump came the reply.

"Oh, very funny" said Bill, "Never mind blowing raspberries,

just come down Eric."

Brump!

"That's not Eric" said Santa, "That's Donner, he's got indigestion!"

"So, there's two of them up there?" said Ken.

"No, no Eric's my little helper and Donner is one of the reindeer," said Santa.

Bill and Ken started laughing, "Yes of course they are!"

By this time, Eric and all the reindeer were peering over the edge of the roof at what was going on down below.

Prancer and Dancer looked at each other and grinned, then both said together "PARTY TIME!"

Prancer nodded his antlers at the snowman and a strange shimmering light surrounded the snowman.

The snowman shook his head, then put his hand up to adjust his sunglasses, looking over at the police car.

He said to himself,

"Hey man, check the hot wheels!"

Santa by this time realised things were not going well.

"Look" he said, "I can prove it, look up there,

there's Eric and all the reindeer."

Bill and Ken looked up but could only see a

snow-covered roof.

"Oh yes, of course there is," said Bill.

"Eric, Rudolph, tell them who I am" shouted Santa,

who by this time was getting quite worried?

"They can't see us, said Cupid only you can, what on earth

have you been up to?

Oh, my headaches getting worse" said Cupid,

Brump, "My indigestion's getting worse," said Donner.

"Cor can't you face the other way?" said Blitzson.

Brump, "My doze", "My head!".

Bill and Ken had seen enough, "Okay Bill," said Ken "You check round the back and I'll take Santa here, back to the car."

"Okay" said Bill and off he went.

"Right, you're under arrest and I'm taking you to Picton Police Station."

Ken walked Santa, still protesting, over to where the police car should have been.

He looked up and down the lane, but it had gone!

Cupid looked across at Dancer and Prancer

"What have you two been up to?" said Cupid.

"Nothing" said Prancer and Dancer together.

Cupid looked around the garden,

then turned in horror to Prancer,

"What have you done with the snowman?" he shouted.

Prancer and Dancer looked at each other.

"You tell him "said Dancer "No you" said Prancer,

"Oh, alright then.

The snowman drove off in the police car," said Dancer.

"Hey cool dude," said Comet.

Cupid turned to Eric "Have you found that stardust yet?

I can't keep up with all this."

"I'm trying said Eric. Rudolph wants nose cream,

Blitzson wants a peg for his nose, and you want stardust.

I can only be in ten places at the same time!"

Out at the front, Ken was still looking for the police car.

Santa stood next to him wondering what to do next.

"Eric, ERIC ! Do something!" shouted Santa.

Meanwhile, Bill was checking round the back.

All seemed Okay, except for a strange raspberry sound coming from the roof.

Brump, "Must be the wind" he thought to himself.

He made his way back round to the front, past the fishpond, when something made him stop.

There seemed to be a strange glow around the fishpond.

Suddenly, Norman the gnome's fishing rod line gave a little tug, followed by a jerk Norman was pulled into the fishpond, with a great splash as he hit the water.

At this point, Nobby started laughing his head off.

"Ooooh ha ha, ooooh ha ha."

Bill stood motionless with his mouth wide open when there was a shout of "Whoooah"!

 Norman was swimming for all his worth, as a shark's fin chased him out of the water.

Nobby laughed even more, but Norman couldn't see the funny side of it at all.

"I suppose you think that's funny, do you?" said Norman.

"Hilarious" said Nobby "Oooh ha ha!"

Norman walked over and broke his fishing rod over Nobby's head.

"Now laugh, you great lump of stone," said Norman.

"I can't help it" said Nobby,

as he punched Norman with a clunk.

"Oooh, that was funny, ha ha!"

Bill stood motionless as the two concrete gnomes started fighting around the pond.

The shark was still swimming up and down the pond when it suddenly leapt out of the water and bit the bum out of Nobby's trousers!

At this point, Bill decided to make a run for it.

much to the delight of Prancer and Dancer who were laughing like a couple of naughty schoolboys.

Bill ran back to Ken and said "Slap me. Go on, slap me!"

Ken slapped Bill who shouted "Aaagh, that hurt.

Oh, no I'm not dreaming, I must be going mad then.

Where's the car, let's get out of here."

"I don't know, said Ken. I left it here"

"Err the snowman's got it" said Santa quietly.

"Oh no, this is all I need, a mad burglar and for Pete's' sake, take that ridiculous beard off," said Bill.

"Aaagh" went Santa as Bill pulled at Santa's beard.

"Blimey, it's real," said Bill.

"Of course, it's real," said Santa.

At this point a car could be heard coming down the lane.

Bill dashed out into the lane. "It's our car" said Bill,

He jumped out waving his arms.

The police car pulled up at the gate,

"Aaagh" went Bill, "There's a snowman driving our car."

The driver's window was open, and the snowman was resting his elbow on the door.

Bill shouted, "Get out of our car or you're under arrest."

The snowman adjusted his sunglasses

"Hey, chill out man. I was just cruising the wheels,"

He flicked a switch "And dig these crazy horns"

DEE DAA, DEE DAA.

"GET HIM OUT," shouted Ken.

"Don't worry, I'll get him out," said Santa.

He shut his eyes and there was a strange crackling sound,

followed by a loud thud as both front doors fell off the police car.

"Hey man, you've trashed my wheels" said the snowman getting out of the car.

"No, no, this isn't happening," said Bill.

"Don't worry, I'll put it right," said Santa.

He shut his eyes again, there was a funny rumbling sound. They all looked round to see a small wooden garden windmill start to turn, getting faster and faster.

Prancer and Dancer on the roof, were crying with laughter at what was happening down below.

"Hey, hey, watch this," said Dancer.

He put on a silly voice

"Windmill one, you are clear for take-off."

The windmill gathered speed and slowly rose into the air and started flying around the garden.

Prancer laughed "That's nothing, watch this!"

A large fir tree in a flower tub by the front door, began to shake and rumble then suddenly blasted off

The fir tree shot down the windmill, which crashed into next doors garden and burst into flames.

Bill land Ken stood in the front garden in a daze,

not knowing what to do.

Meanwhile, Donner was still brumping up on the roof.

Nobby and Norman were still fighting around the pond and

Santa had just made the headlights fall off the police car.

"Okay, that's it, you're all under arrest," shouted Bill.

"You can't arrest a snowman," said Ken.

The snowman walked over to Bill and put one hand on his shoulder.

"Hey, chill out man, it's cool!" said the snowman,

Who then walked off towards the tool shed.

"Hey, come back, you're under arrest," shouted Bill.

"Pull yourself together, you're talking to a snowman," said Ken.

"Oh, yeah and you're holding Santa Claus," shouted Bill.

"Lads, lads, calm down, I can put everything right," said Santa.

"No don't do anything, look at our car," said Bill.

"Trust me," said Santa.

"This should be good," said Dancer.

"It will with a bit of help," said Prancer.

"No stop it," shouted Cupid.

The police car started to shake,

then disappeared in a puff of smoke.

Everyone looked into the lane and as the smoke cleared,

There standing where the police car had been,

was a hot dog van with a blue flashing light on top, and a blue & red stripe down the side.

"Oooh, I'll have a jumbo whopper and a bucket of chips", Brump went Donner. "COSMIC" said Comet

"Ooops" said Santa.

"Eric, find that stardust quick," said Cupid.

"I'm dreaming, this is all a bad dream and I'm going to wake up in a minute and it's all going to be alright," said Bill.

"Things can't get any worse," said Ken.

But no sooner had he said it, an engine could be heard starting in the tool shed.

Then suddenly, the door burst open, and the snowman came roaring out on the ride-on lawn mower.

"Dig the crazy wheels" he said, as he shot past Bill and Ken and disappeared down the lane.

"That's it, I'm after the snowman" said Bill,

He ran out and jumped into the hot dog van.

Ken looked round the garden, the shark was still swimming up and down the pond.

Nobby and Norman had knocked each other out.

The windmill lay in next doors garden, on fire, having been shot down by a fir tree.

Santa stood next to Ken wondering what to do next.

Ken looked at the hot dog van and shouted, "Wait for me".

He ran and jumped into the hot dog van with Bill,
Santa followed shouting "What about me?

 Do you want any help?"

"No, no. Go away, clear off" shouted Ken as they sped off down the lane throwing hot dog rolls at Santa.

"What about my jumbo whopper?" shouted Donner.

Santa stood in the garden alone.

It had all gone quiet, and he was wondering what to do.

Suddenly, there was a huge shout from Eric

"I'VE FOUND IT!" he said, and he thrust his arm in the air

holding a glistening bag of stardust.

"Oh poo" said Dancer, just when we were having fun.

"Right lads, let's get out of here quick," said Cupid.

He nodded his antlers at Santa and with a

"Puff" Santa was back in his sleigh.

"WHOOAH, I still can't get used to that," said Santa

"Still come on lads all into position, everybody ready?"
"Yes, yes. all okay", Brump went Donner.

Santa took up the reigns "YEE HAAR giddy up"

shouted Santa, and off they went into the night sky.

"We must stop him watching all those cowboy films,"

said Cupid.

Santa circled the cottages as Eric sprinkled stardust over the back of the sleigh, which fell over the cottages.

"Now off to catch up with the snowman and put that right," said Santa.

Katie and Kevin woke early next morning and ran excitedly downstairs.

There under the tree were all their presents.

They sat on Mums special Chinese rug and excitedly opened them all.

Later in the day, they both put on their coats and hats, pulled on their wellingtons and went outside, to wish the snowman a Merry Christmas.

The snowman stood on guard in the middle of the lawn and the windmill was back in its right place.

Katie went over to the fishpond

to check on the fish and give them some food.

She stopped and picked up Norman the gnome

who was back on his toadstool.

"Dad, what's on his face?" said Katie.

Mr. Robinson looked at him,

"Funny, it looks like a black eye!"

About the author

As a child of the 50's I was brought up on the television programmes of Mr Pastry, The Marx Bros, Laurel & Hardy, Charlie Chaplin & many more.
Which is where my love of slapstick and the absurd comes from.

I get the biggest thrill from making people smile. With my writing, I hope to entertain, not just children but anyone who is still a kid inside.

https://www.glyndaviesbooks.com

Acknowledgments

I want to say a special thanks to the people who have assisted me in producing this book

Robin Davies

For his time in creating the front & rear cover artwork

https://www.robindaviesillustration.com

Sarha Khan

For editing my ramblings into a printable book

Graham Mack

For narrating and producing a brilliant audible version

https://www.grahammack.com/

You dear reader

Thank you for buying this book, I hope it makes you smile

Printed in Great Britain
by Amazon